PRAISE FOR
AUTUMN MOONBEAM: DANCE MAGIC!

'Autumn Moonbeam is such an endearing and enthusiastic
protagonist. The imaginative witchy world Emma has
created tackles magic in a fresh new way; full of charm,
friendship and lots of sweet-smelling spells! Paired with
Heidi Cannon's stunning illustrations that burst with
energy, Autumn Moonbeam is the perfect read for fans of
the Isadora Moon and The Worst Witch. There really is a
sparkle on every page.' LAURA ELLEN ANDERSON

'A warm-hearted story, sparkling with magic
and dance.' TAMSIN MORI

'An acrobatic delight of a story.' ABI ELPHINSTONE

'As a child dancer, gymnast, and lover of all things witchy,
this book would have undoubtedly been top of my read
again pile! Whimsical, joyful, and inventive. A beam
of sunshine. And complemented by the most
gorgeous illustrations.' KATE FOSTER

'Perfect for kids who love fantasy and keeping active,
complete with a magical dance routine to learn.'
SKYE MCKENNA

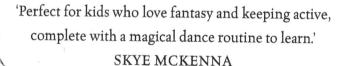

'Take one nervous witch, a dash of dance, a splash of
humour, oodles of warmth and you have all the perfect
ingredients for a magical new adventure. Wonderfully
diverse and effortlessly entertaining, the story just leaps
off the page demanding to be read. *Autumn Moonbeam*
is a charming and lively debut that is bound to
delight younger readers with its sparkling prose and
engaging illustrations. I loved it!' JO CLARKE

'Magically joyful and full of sparkle.'
SERENA PATEL

'Full of fun and bouncing with charm – *Autumn Moonbeam*
is wickedly good! TAMSYN MURRAY

'A spelltacular, dancetastic story with magical illustrations
from Heidi Cannon. I know a lot of children who will be
keenly building their Autumn Moonbeam collection!'
EMILY KENNY

'Filled with warmth, humour and magical fun. It's packed with witty puns and wonderful relatable witchy characters. The illustrations by Heidi Cannon are playful and inviting. It's an absolute joy to read.' TAMSIN COOKE

'It will have little readers dancing with joy.' PERDITA CARGILL

'A sparkling new series, I can't wait to see what's next for Autumn!' ANDY SHEPHERD

'Flaming frogs' bottoms! Autumn Moonbeam is exactly the joyous series of stories I would have adored as a child. Charming, exciting and full of magical fun.' SWAPNA REDDY

Joyful, fun and playful it just carries the reader on a magical journey of adventures.' CAMILLA CHESTER

'It'll make your budding dancers hop, skip and cartwheel with delight. A spooky, sparkly five stars!' LUCY BRANDT

'A lovely book brimming with joy . . . perfect for little ones who love magic and dance.' HANNAH GOLD

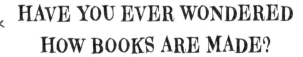

HAVE YOU EVER WONDERED
HOW BOOKS ARE MADE?

UCLan Publishing is an award winning independent publisher specialising in Children's and Young Adult books. Based at The University of Central Lancashire, this Preston-based publisher teaches MA Publishing students how to become industry professionals using the content and resources from its business; students are included at every stage of the publishing process and credited for the work that they contribute.

The business doesn't just help publishing students though. UCLan Publishing has supported the employability and real-life work skills for the University's Illustration, Acting, Translation, Animation, Photography, Film & TV students and many more. This is the beauty of books and stories; they fuel many other creative industries! The MA Publishing students are able to get involved from day one with the business and they acquire a behind the scenes experience of what it is like to work for a such a reputable independent.

The MA course was awarded a Times Higher Award (2018) for Innovation in the Arts and the business, UCLan Publishing, was awarded Best Newcomer at the Independent Publishing Guild (2019) for the ethos of teaching publishing using a commercial publishing house. As the business continues to grow, so too does the student experience upon entering this dynamic Masters course.

www.uclanpublishing.com
www.uclanpublishing.com/courses/
uclanpublishing@uclan.ac.uk

For my friend and writing buddy, Tizzie,
who helped me follow my dreams.

Autumn Moonbeam: Spooky Sleepover is a uclanpublishing book

First published in Great Britain in 2022 by
uclanpublishing
University of Central Lancashire
Preston, PR1 2HE, UK

Text copyright © Emma Finlayson-Palmer, 2022
Illustrations copyright © Heidi Cannon, 2022

978-1-912979-92-9

1 3 5 7 9 10 8 6 4 2

Set in 14/22pt Celestia Antiqua MVB

A CIP catalogue record for this book is available from the British Library.

Printed and bound in Great Britain by Clays Ltd, Elcograf S.p.A.

AUTUMN

MOONBEAM

SPOOKY SLEEPOVER!

EMMA FINLAYSON-PALMER & HEIDI CANNON

uclanpublishing

AUTUMN MOONBEAM

KNOTWEED MOONBEAM

STORM

MORDECAI AND
TOADFLAX MOONBEAM

SILVER MOONBEAM
(AKA MUM)

GHOSTLY
GRAN

TREVOR

ZEPHYR MOONBEAM

EDITH 'BATTY' BATTINGTON

SEVERINA BLOODWORTH

LEIF KERRSE

MR SNAIL CRUNCHER

MISS SPINNING WEB

ONYX DARKSTONE

COSMIC

VERITY CHARM

SKYE
CLOUDSKIPPER

RAINBOW
CLOUDSKIPPER

SPARKLEDALE
DANCE ACADEMY

AUTUMN MOONBEAM kicked her legs into a handstand, as strands of green sparkly light swirled around in her bedroom.

Zephyr, Autumn's twin, was propped up against her pillows reading a book. She was already dressed, with her hair coiled into two tight plaits. "Why are you up so early on a Saturday?" Zephyr groaned from the bottom bunk bed.

"It's my first day at Sparkledale Dance Academy!" Autumn dropped down into a bridge and pink and purple lights twinkled in an arch over her. Then she stood up, arms stretched skywards, as if she was performing to a room full of other witches, and not just her sister and Storm, her tabby cat.

Storm trotted after Autumn as she skipped from her room and slid down the banister.

"Morning!" Autumn called, as she carefully dodged Ghostly Gran, who was floating at the bottom of the stairs blowing dust from pictures and moving things around the hall. It was freezing if you accidentally fell through her, and Autumn didn't want to start the day feeling like she'd had an ice bath.

Autumn dodged a piece of slug slime on toast that flew in her direction and splodged down the wall. Her two older brothers, Mordecai and Toadflax, were flicking breakfast at each other in the kitchen. She loved her amazing family, but her brothers always got in her way when she was practising her dance magic.

Autumn poured herself some Lice Crispies, stretching her leg up on the kitchen counter as she ate the cereal.

"Dance! Dance!" Knotweed called, as he toddled into the kitchen with Trevor the baby dragon who was hiccupping little wisps of smoke. Knotweed was Autumn's younger brother and she smiled as he spun enthusiastically round in circles, creating orange sparkles of dance magic, before falling on his bottom and burping.

"That's right, Weed, Autumn is dancing today," Mum said, scooping him up. "We'll have to get going soon, you don't want to be late."

Autumn felt a mixture of nerves and excitement and struggled to swallow her Lice Crispies. She'd been so excited to start at Sparkledale, but now she was worried she wouldn't be good enough. *Maybe Verity made a mistake in choosing me for the team*, she thought.

Verity, the head coach and owner of Sparkledale, had called Autumn on the magical mirror a week before, and offered her a place on the competitive dance team, Black Cats.

Mum held Weed under one arm as he squirmed and wriggled. "Right then, are we ready for the off?"

✳ ✳ ✳

Autumn's tummy cartwheeled as she stood outside Sparkledale Dance Academy. An animation of a witch backflipping over shimmering silver and turquoise letters welcomed them on a sign above the doors.

"I'm so excited!" Edith Battingham, Autumn's best friend who everyone always called Batty, nudged her arm.

"Yeah, me too." Autumn gulped, pushing down the moths fluttering around her chest.

"Good luck, Pumpkin!" Mum said.

Autumn's cheeks flushed. "Thanks," she said, checking over her shoulder to make sure no one else had heard her mum use her special nickname.

"You'll be absolutely fine; you've been doing gymnastics and dance since you started at Pointy Hat Primary school." Mum smiled.

"But this isn't a normal class, I'm training to perform in front of other witches and at competitions." Autumn chewed her lip.

"Ooh, I'm sooo proud of you! And you too, Batty!" Mum beamed.

"Thank you, Mrs Moonbeam." Batty grinned, and it looked like her bat-shaped birthmark was taking flight on her cheek.

Autumn took a deep breath then pushed open the doors and walked into the academy. It was cool inside, and she was greeted by lots of nervous and smiling faces.

I *can't believe I'm finally a member of Sparkledale,* Autumn thought.

Everyone wore matching midnight-grey tops; purple sequins spelt out their team name, *Black Cats,* and across the back in turquoise sequins was the club name – *Sparkledale.*

"Autumn! Batty!" Leif Kerrse, one of their best friends from school, was already there. "Isn't this great? Our first time training together as a team!" Leif hugged his friends.

"Hello!" said a small witch Autumn recognised from the year below at school. Her hair swished in a high ponytail as she bounced over to them.

※ 9 ※

Leif introduced her to Autumn and Batty. "Hey everybody, this is Skye. She's an amazing tumbler."

Autumn remembered seeing Skye doing brilliant moves across the school playground, surrounded by swirls of magical glitter and butterflies.

"Good morning, everyone," Verity said, throwing her arms out to beckon them closer. "It's wonderful to see our new team members today. Let's give everyone a big Black Cats welcome!"

Cheers and shouts echoed around the room.

"Fabulous! Now, let's get warmed up. I can't wait to start teaching you the new dance routine." Verity clicked her fingers and the gym doors opened wide.

Even though she had seen it at try outs, Autumn was amazed as she looked around the gym at the winning trophies and banners lining the walls. One whole wall was a big mirror so they could watch themselves as they danced. Cosmic,

the club cat and mascot, wove his way around the room and rubbed against Autumn's leg.

"Hello, Cosmic." She stroked him behind his ear, and he purred happily.

MEOWFFFTZZZ!

Cosmic's fur stood on end as the door to the gym clattered open. Severina Bloodworth, Autumn's snooty neighbour and classmate, stood in the doorway. She flicked her dark, long hair over her shoulder – her locks had been curled and were very fluffy and shiny. "Sorry, I'm late. I was getting my hair done."

Autumn remembered how Severina had turned up late to try outs the previous week. *Typical Severina behaviour*, she thought.

BATWING AND
MOON-FLOP

VERITY STOOD with her hands on her hips. "Don't make being late a regular thing, Severina. Part of being a sportsperson is being a good timekeeper too."

"I didn't think the appointment would take so long. They used all the best potions and spells." Severina swished her hair like she was in an advert.

Autumn rolled her eyes. This was so typical

of Severina – holding up the whole class. Cosmic's fur was still standing on end as he curled inside his favourite trophy for a nap.

"Now we're all here, I've got an exciting announcement to make," Verity said, and all eyes in the room were now on her. "Teamwork makes the dream work. So . . ." Verity paused for dramatic effect. "I have arranged a team bonding sleepover in the gym in two weeks."

There were whoops of excitement and cheering.

"This is going to be so much fun!" Skye hovered above the mats as her wings fluttered excitedly.

"I can wear my unicorn onesie!" Leif said, with a huge grin.

"We can have a witching-hour feast with snot chocolate and star sprinkles," Batty said.

Autumn smiled at her friends; excitement and nerves fluttered in her chest. She'd never stayed away from home overnight before, but she really wanted to be there with her teammates.

"OK," said Verity, "get warmed up and jump in line."

There was a large pile of mats at one end of the gym and a long inflatable runway called a tumble track. One of the coaches, Rainbow, was already bounding down the track doing a type of gymnastics called tumbling.

Rainbow ran, hopped, then put her hands

down like she was doing a handstand. She was a blur of movement as she launched her legs into the air, pushed them forward, and landed before straightening up again. Butterflies and birds circled around her and she breathed in the smell of a bright, sunny day.

"Wow!" Autumn gasped. "She's magical!"

"Front handspring," Rainbow announced to the team. "One of my favourite tumbling moves."

Skye was next to Autumn, twirling a piece of her long blue hair around her finger. "Rainbow's my sister. She's always bouncing about like that; she never stays still."

Autumn thought Skye must be the same as she fidgeted and hopped from foot to foot.

"I hope I can learn to do that." Autumn swallowed nervously, her throat suddenly dry. She stared at Batty in panic, all her confidence melting away. *What if I'm not good enough?* she thought.

What if I let the team down? "I'm going! I've changed my mind!"

Batty grabbed Autumn's arm. "Why would you change your mind?"

Autumn looked towards the door. "What if I can't do it?"

"If you weren't good enough, you'd never have been picked. You've always wanted to join the competitive team."

Autumn knew Batty was right. Joining Sparkledale had been her dream for ages. She straightened up and pushed her shoulders back. *I can do this.*

As they followed Verity's instructions and went through a series of cartwheels and front walkovers. Puffs of sparkly clouds floated up from dancers when it went well, and dark clouds when they were wobbly. Autumn heard Severina huffing and puffing further down the line.

"Eeeek!" Severina squealed, tripping over her own feet and crashing into the witch next to her.

It's not like Severina to be so clumsy, Autumn thought. Normally Severina was one of the best . . . at everything!

"OK, everyone hold still a moment," Verity

instructed. "Severina, as lovely as your hair is, it's getting in your eyes. If you haven't got a hair tie with you, there's a tub of new ones in the storage cupboard – help yourself."

Severina stomped out of the gym, her curls bouncing.

Verity clapped her hands for attention. "This is a good time to take a water break."

Batty shook her head as she walked over to the water bottles. "Dancing dragons, why does Severina always have to show off?"

"Her hair does look really nice though," Autumn said, thinking about her own mass of curls that took some special magic to get tied up for training. *How does Zephyr always manage to get her hair into such neat plaits?* she wondered. *We have the same sort of hair but mine never looks that tidy.*

"You know I used to really dislike my hair?" Leif said, before taking a big gulp of water.

"Really?" Skye asked.

"Yeah, until I realised it was *growing* on me – get it?" Leif laughed, while his friends groaned at the joke.

Severina reappeared in the gym, her hair pulled back in a high ponytail, her scowl clearly visible. She had a drink from her Number One Dancer bottle then lined up ready to start work again. She didn't look at any of the other witches.

Perhaps she's feeling embarrassed, Autumn thought, *I know I'd hate everyone looking at me.*

As they started to dance, all the water bottles behind them fell over and rolled around the gym floor.

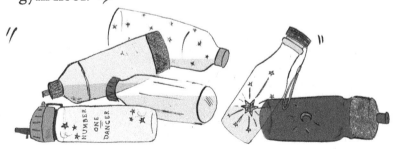

"What the . . . ?" Batty said, scrunching her nose in confusion.

"OK, settle down. It was probably a gust of air or something." Verity swished her finger and each bottle stopped moving then stood upright again.

"Onyx, could you do the honours and magic up a demonstration, please?" Verity asked.

"*Sparkle and prance, turn on the spot and perfect your dance!*" Onyx chanted, and a sparkly holographic figure appeared in a very straight pose – lining up their feet before pivoting and turning on the spot.

"Getting the basics in place like you saw in the demonstration will make for the best performances," Verity said.

Autumn and the rest of Black Cats followed the moves, and she tried to get her feet lined up just right before turning on the spot. Her twist was followed by a thin thread of magic that looked like a pink ribbon fluttering around her ankles. A loud crash from the corner of the gym startled Autumn and the pink ribbon suddenly tightened around her ankles causing her to tumble to the floor.

"Ouch." Autumn rubbed her elbow and looked around and saw quite a few people on the ground, looking confused.

"How peculiar," Verity said, inspecting a trophy that had fallen from a shelf. Cosmic meowed at her side and sniffed the air. "You can't smell any magic then, Cosmic?"

He sat down and cleaned his paws, showing that he wasn't worried that someone had been casting spells when they shouldn't.

The team got back to work and as the first few moves became easier with practise there were snowflakes and silver sparkles fluttering around them. Moving in harmony as a team created a beautiful mini snowstorm of magic inside the gym. The air above the dancers sparkled and swirled.

Autumn was sure she could hear Severina whispering "go away!" but then a loud noise made her jump. It was like someone blowing a raspberry and it broke the magic that their dancing had created. Snowflakes melted and caused a rain shower above the dancers.

"That's freezing!" Autumn said, shivering and rubbing her arms.

"I'm a little disappointed that someone here has been blowing raspberries like that. I should hope there are no fall outs between friends and teammates." Verity had her hands on her hips as she stared around the gym at the now cold and soggy dancers. "*Warm air fly, make these dancers dry!*"

Verity chanted, and the smell of freshly washed clothes filled the air.

A blast of warm rushed over the dancers. Autumn felt her T-shirt and it was dry again, the sequins twinkled across the front.

"I wouldn't put it past Severina to have done this," said Batty.

"But she got wet too," Autumn said.

"You know what she's like though." Batty folded her arms and stared at Severina.

"What are you looking at Batwing and Moon-flop?" Severina sneered.

"See!" said Batty.

"What's all this tension about?" Verity asked.

"Nothing, Miss Charm." Severina smiled sweetly. "Thank you for lending me the hair tie."

"That's quite alright. Just make sure you turn up to practise next week with your hair out of your eyes." Verity smiled.

Autumn wasn't sure if Severina was up to something or not. There was definitely weird stuff happening at the gym. But Autumn *was* sure of one thing . . . she was excited that she was finally a member of Sparkledale Dance Academy!

FLAPPING
FAIRY WINGS!

"**A**NSWER THE DOOR!" shrieked the enchanted
doorbell at Autumn's house.

Autumn opened the door and Batty, Leif and
Skye were all smiling at her. "Hi!" Autumn said,
inviting them inside. "Sorry about my noisy
brothers. They are so embarrassing."

Mordecai and Toadflax were arguing over the
spell-a-vision in the living room. They were now

rolling around the floor wrestling for control of the handset.

"Boys! Stop that now!" Mum shouted from the kitchen. "You're not too big for time out you know."

Autumn and her friends stifled their giggles as her brothers looked red-faced and frowned. Walking through the house they saw Mum painting in the kitchen, with Weed and Trevor covered in paint and creating their own artwork on a big piece of paper on the floor – Trevor had already singed part of the paper and eaten a paintbrush. Meanwhile, Zephyr was sitting at the table doing her homework.

"Hello, everyone!" Mum said. "Watch out for paint, we're having some creative time."

"Looks like fun, Mrs Moonbeam," Batty said.

"We're going in the garden," Autumn announced.

"I might join you. I can't concentrate in the kitchen." Zephyr scooped up her work and followed Autumn and the others into the garden. Storm rushed out alongside them, dodging paint that was flying off the end of Trevor's tail.

"Do you want to join in with our dancing?" Skye asked, pirouetting on the spot.

"Erm, no thanks," said Zephyr. "Lots of work to do." She wiggled a pen and notebook, and numbers fluttered in the air above her. Storm leapt and tried to catch one, then gave up and plonked himself down on one of Zephyr's books.

"Zephyr prefers puzzles and numbers to backflips and cartwheels," Leif explained.

The friends went over some of the moves they'd been learning at Sparkledale Dance Academy. They were already getting pretty good at working together as a group.

"How about you magic up that weboline, so we can have a stretchy floor to bounce on, Autumn?" Batty asked.

"I've got a better idea!" Autumn flourished her

wand and chanted. "*Abracadoodle, bibbity back, give me a thing like a tumbling track!*"

The sickly-sweet smell of toffee apples filled the air and blue sparkles flew out from her wand. Long, thin glistening strands wove around and around until they formed a long track similar to the one in the gym.

"Flapping fairy wings! That's brilliant!" Skye said, fluttering her own wings a little.

They tried the moves again, now with extra spring and bounce in their steps, and sparkly snowflakes fluttered above them – with the occasional hail stone when one of them made a wrong move. When it went right, there was a smell of cinnamon in the air that reminded them of sweet sticky howling-buns.

 "What's this? The getting-it-wrong club?" Severina poked her nose over the fence. "I can do that better. Watch this," she said, before she bounded on to the stage she had set up for dancing in her garden.

"She's always so rude," Batty said.

The friends moved closer to the fence to get a better look. Severina moved gracefully and snowflakes fluttered and twirled around her like she was inside a snow globe.

"I hate to admit it, but she is really good," said Autumn.

 Severina overheard. "I'm not just good, I'm amazing!" she replied, before performing a cartwheel which went straight into a

back handspring and looked like she was doing a handstand into a bridge. Swirls of colourful magic swished around her.

As Severina stood up, she looked really nervous.

"I've got to go, see you losers later." She rushed inside her house.

"What was that all about?" Batty asked.

"I think I know why." Autumn pointed to where Ghostly Gran was hovering near the back door.

Batty explained, while trying not to laugh, that last time Severina was showing off, Gran had floated right through the fence and given her a cold shock.

"Don't you think it's a bit weird that things kept going wrong at dance class today after Severina arrived?" Leif asked.

"I thought that, but would she really do magic that affects her too?" Autumn said.

"Well, she turned you into a black cat at try outs," Batty said.

Skye gasped. "Did she really? I'm surprised Verity let her join the team."

"I covered for her a little. She's not all bad," Autumn said, remembering how nice Severina had been to her before they knew they'd both got a place at Sparkledale.

"I still think she could have caused the trouble

today." Batty frowned. "Anyway, let's forget about Severina now and dance instead."

The friends laughed and danced but a little knot of worry formed in Autumn's chest. The more she thought about it, the more she wondered if Severina was back to her old tricks at the gym.

TROUBLE AND TROPHIES

INSIDE THE gym at Sparkledale Dance Academy, Cosmic was looking very grumpy.

"You'll have to excuse Cosmic today; I'm afraid he's in a bad mood," Verity said.

"Why?" Batty asked.

Onyx pointed to an empty space on the shelf where Cosmic's favourite sleeping trophy used to be. "It's vanished!"

There were mutters and gasps around the gym.

"Who would take a trophy?" Autumn whispered to Batty.

"I bet it's Severina," said Batty.

"But she must have lots of her own?" Autumn asked. "Where is she, anyway?" Autumn glanced around, sure that she had seen Severina arrive when she had.

"Probably to get back at Cosmic for sniffing out her magic at the try outs – it's exactly the sort of thing she'd do." Batty shrugged.

Verity got everyone warming up and stretching ready to train. Autumn overheard some of the other team members discussing strange goings on at the gym.

Severina appeared from the store cupboard.

She looked away quickly when she spotted Autumn watching and hurried to line up and start stretching.

What's she up to now? Autumn wondered and looked round at Batty to see if she'd spotted Severina looking uncomfortable too.

"Told you," Batty whispered. "Bet she's hidden the trophy in the cupboard."

Cosmic stalked around the edge of the gym whilst Autumn and the rest of her team started learning new moves and sequences to add to their routine.

"Let's go through those moves again – just listen to my count." Verity looked around the gym. "On the count of one, I want you to step to the left, then on two, step to the right, then three, pivot on the spot," Verity instructed.

Autumn followed each move, biting her lip as she concentrated.

"One ... two and three pivot round ... four, arms

bent, fists clenched like you're holding a broomstick ... body roll, five ... grapevine ... step to the side, other leg back, side, tap. Other way ... six ... side, back, side. Don't cross in front. Side, behind, side, tap. Side, behind, side, and pose!" Verity instructed.

Rainbow also went through the moves at the front of the group with Verity so Autumn and the rest of Black Cats could follow.

"Now, you have it. Take it up to tempo. Not too much faster, but just to get the flow of the grapevine. OK? Onyx could you hit the music, please?" Verity said.

As the music began, the sound vibrated through the floor rippling up through Autumn's body.

"And one ... two ... three ... four ..." Verity counted them through each step.

Autumn felt like she was made of every colour sparkle as happiness at dancing beamed from her.

"Five . . . six . . . seven . . . eight . . . pose! Wooooh!" Verity cheered. "Put everything together now and add in your front handsprings and cartwheels too."

Autumn was mid-cartwheel when she noticed the photo wall. *Flaming frogs' bottoms,* she thought, *what's going on?* Each team picture on the wall was spinning round. The sparkly butterflies of dance magic that had been spiralling around Autumn popped like balloons and left a smell like rotten eggs hanging in the air as she fell over.

"What's up, Autumn? Cartwheels aren't usually a problem for you." Rainbow fluttered by her side and helped her back up.

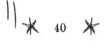

"It's the pictures," Autumn said, pointing at the wall.

"Oh!" Rainbow practically squeaked. "Erm, Verity? I think there's something a little odd going on here."

Every last one of the team photos on the wall was now upside down or at an angle. Cosmic hissed.

"What is it, Cosmic? Is some witch playing a little joke on us?" She waved her wand over the pictures until they were all back as they should be, with athletes smiling from the frames. "No tricks and nonsense now team, not if you want the sleepover to go ahead next week." Verity frowned.

"Look who is biting her nails," Leif said, nudging Autumn.

Autumn had never seen Severina doing *that*

before. How odd, she thought. Has Severina got something to feel nervous about? It really isn't looking good for Severina being innocent.

MAGICAL CREATURES

IT WAS Monday, and Autumn was excited to talk to her friends about the sleepover at the gym. Autumn zoomed and looped on her broomstick thinking about all the fun things they could do. Zephyr flew alongside with her headphones on listening to a book about Ancient Greek mathematicians. Every so often Zephyr would mutter something, and numbers and symbols would circle around her head before floating away like clouds.

They had just parked their broomsticks in the shed outside Pointy Hat Primary when Leif and Batty pulled up.

Batty's eyes were as round as cauldrons as she talked about all the different things they could do at the sleepover. "I can bring my *Witches of Dance and Gym* cards. I have a whole new collection for the Paraaarghlympians. Did you see the Paraaarghlympic dance team on the spell-a-vison at the weekend? They were magical!" she said dreamily.

"They created a display with water and fire whirling around each other. It was brilliant!" Leif added.

"Maybe one day we could be that good if we keep training with Sparkledale," Autumn said.

"Well, you know what Verity always says..." Leif waited for everyone to join in with him.

"*Teamwork makes the dream work!*" The friends said in unison.

"Come on now, hurry along – it's time for class, not chanting," Mr Snailcruncher, their teacher said as they walked up the corridor.

The Magical Creatures teacher, Mrs Featherton, often had animals in the classroom for practical demonstrations and for learning how to treat the creatures properly. After PE, Magical Creatures was Autumn's favourite lesson. The Magical Creatures classroom always smelt a bit like a zoo. A strange mixture of animal food and poo.

Mr Snailcruncher entered the classroom and closed the door behind him. Everyone looked around confused. Autumn checked they weren't accidentally in the Potions class, which was where Mr Snailcruncher could usually be found.

"Mrs Featherton is off ill today, so I'll be covering her class," Mr Snailcruncher announced, and some witches groaned.

Severina put her hand up.

"Yes, Miss Bloodworth?" Mr Snailcruncher raised his eyebrows, so it looked like two hairy caterpillars were wriggling along the top of his glasses.

"Sir, we've been learning all about fiery creatures, and Mrs Featherton said we would be looking at phoenixes next," Severina said.

"Well, when she's back I'm sure she can continue. But for today turn to page eighty-eight in your Magical Creatures handbooks and we'll have a look at things that are either see-through or can turn invisible."

"But that's impossible!" Leif said.

"What are you talking about, Leif?" Mr Snailcruncher's caterpillar eyebrows were squidged together in a frown now.

"You said we will *look*, but you can't *look* at them if they're invisible," Leif said, and there was giggling around the classroom.

"Very funny, now get on with what you're supposed to be doing – unless you'd like to see the headteacher?"

Leif opened his book quickly. *Poor Leif*, Autumn thought. He just couldn't help himself and usually said whatever he was thinking.

Autumn read a list on page eighty-eight of all sorts of creatures who were either invisible or could turn invisible, and information on each. *Ghosts*, she knew all about that one with Gran still floating around. When she first turned up nobody even realised until Mum spilt a tin of paint on her. She was much easier to spot after that.

There were all sorts of animals that could camouflage, almost as if they were invisible, by blending into their background. Autumn needed to remember this for future potions where they turned into animals.

Autumn spotted a paragraph that made hairs on her neck stand on end.

PIXIES

Pixies, well known for their mischief, are sometimes known to turn invisible and cause trouble. They especially like to hide in places where there will be lots of people so they can move their things and turn items upside down.

Autumn realised this was just what had been happening in the gym. It *has to be a pixie*, she thought. She continued reading . . .

Anti-pixie mischief remedies include wearing your clothes inside out and carrying bells with you.

Bells? Autumn thought, *it might look a little odd, but I guess it could be worth a try.* She glanced across the classroom at Severina, who spotted her and stuck her tongue out. Autumn rolled her eyes, feeling confident that she'd worked out what was going on at the gym.

JINGLE BELLS

INSIDE THE Sparkledale Dance Academy the Black Cats team gathered with their sleeping bags in the gym. Autumn was excited to be back at the dance school so late in the day, but her tummy also fluttered with moths at the thought of being away from home for a whole night.

"I'm soooo excited! This is going to be so much fun!" Skye fluttered over and twirled on the spot next to Autumn and Batty, creating a cloud of bright yellow sparkles that crackled around her and smelt

like popcorn. Skye was wearing a pink fluffy onesie with silvery threads. It had her name across the back in the same glittery stitching.

"Get yourselves settled everyone. To start the evening, I thought you could write each other compliments cards," Verity said.

Autumn lay her sleeping bag and pillow on a mat next to Batty's, the bells on her onesie and bow jingling each time she moved. Autumn smiled at the rest of her team and thought how strange it was to see everyone in their onesies or pyjamas. She was wearing her purple I ♥ Dance onesie.

"*Paper and pens come to me and my team!*" Verity chanted.

Pens zipped through the air like mini broomsticks and the paper fluttered like fairy wings and landed in front of Autumn and her friends.

"Get into groups of four and write your name at the top of your paper and the write something you really want or a goal you want to achieve, then pass it to your left," Verity instructed. "Then the next person needs to write something positive and nice about whoever's paper it is."

Pens scratched against paper and the witches smiled as they passed their notes round, each time writing something new about another teammate.

"When you've gone round the whole group it should have come back to the person it started with. Then we can read them out," said Verity.

Autumn rolled her eyes as Severina stood up, wearing pyjamas with little dancing witches across the fabric, and gold, fluffy slippers. She cleared her throat. "I'll go first . . ."

✳ ✳ ✳

When they'd all finished reading, Autumn smiled so widely her cheeks ached. "I'm going to keep this for ever. I love being part of Black Cats and having magical friends like all of you."

Verity clapped. "Well done, that was a brilliant start to the team bonding sleepover. So wonderful to see you are all learning more about each other and getting to know one another as a team. I'm going to get some snot chocolate warmed up, so have fun for a few minutes."

"I know!" Batty said. "We could tell spooky stories."

Everyone settled themselves in their sleeping bags on the mats.

"What's with the bells, Moon-flop," Severina snorted as she sat down.

"Be quiet, Severina," Autumn mumbled. "I know what you've done."

"What did you say?" Severina didn't sound as confident now.

"I know you are behind the weird things happening each time we dance, and I'm going to prove it."

Severina laughed nervously and moved to sit further away from Autumn.

"What was that all about?" Batty asked.

"Oh, nothing, you know what Severina is like." Autumn didn't want to tell anyone about her pixie idea until she had some proof.

Batty turned the lights off then held her wand under her chin and the glow lit up her face in an eerie way. "I'm going to tell you a story about . . . the gym ghost!"

Autumn wasn't sure she wanted to hear about spooky stories when there were so many strange goings on already.

"A lonely ghost that is said to wail and moan as she dances through the academy," Batty continued.

Then she stood up and twirled, her wand-torch casting flickering shadows across the mirrors and walls in the gym. She tiptoed around, tapping people in the group. Autumn gulped.

"And do you know what?" Batty paused and shone the torch around the room. "The gym ghost is said to haunt this very dance academy!"

Witches gasped and whispered. Autumn thought of her nice safe bed at home with Zephyr in the bunk below and wondered if she should call her mum to collect her.

"This is just silly," Severina said, and folded her arms. "I'm not listening to any more."

"Have you got a better idea?" Batty asked, flicking the light switch on the gym wall.

Autumn felt better with the lights back on and was surprised to find herself agreeing with Severina for once.

"I know." Skye hopped up. "Shall we try our routine?"

Severina huffed but was first up to show off her dancing. Everyone arranged themselves in the lines and placement they would be in if it was training. As they started to dance an eerie *woooooh ooooooooh* noise filled the gym, putting the team off their moves and turning their snowflakes to hailstones that hurt when they landed on them.

"Not again!" Leif groaned.

"What was that?" Batty asked.

"Do you think it's the gym ghost?" Skye whispered.

But before anyone could answer, the winning banners on the walls started flapping wildly as if a strong wind was blowing them.

Autumn looked to Severina who was staring at her feet and looking guilty. *Aha*, she thought. *I knew it – she's been up to something.*

"Eww, that's disgusting," said Leif holding up his water bottle, which was now full of green slime.

"It's the gym ghost!" Skye wailed.

"That's just a made-up story, Skye, don't worry," Batty said.

Autumn hurried over to her bottle; the bells jingling as she moved. "Yuk! Mine is full of gunk too!"

I guess wearing bells hasn't protected me from the pixie after all, Autumn thought. *I knew I should have worn my clothes inside out too!*

"It's you, isn't it, Severina? You're the reason all these things keep happening." Autumn held her water bottle up accusingly.

"No! I didn't do that, I promise," Severina pleaded.

"Hey!" Batty called. "My sleeping bag is inside out, *and* my stuff has been moved."

"How could I do that from over here?" Severina cried. "And look, it's happened to my things too. My clothes are all over the place!"

"Hmm, OK," Autumn said, but she still didn't believe that Severina was telling the whole truth. Even if it wasn't her making weird things happen, Autumn was sure Severina knew who or what was doing it.

SPOOKY SLEEPOVER

HAVE YOU noticed that it's only when we dance that strange things start happening?" Autumn said as the rest of the Black Cats team huddled on the mats.

"I'll do anything, just stop playing tricks on everyone – they all think it's me!"

"I knew it!" Autumn said, and Severina jumped.

"I'm so sorry," Severina suddenly cried. "I never meant for this to happen. It was when I went to get the hair tie on the first day of training. Please don't tell anyone."

"What have you done?" Autumn asked. "Whatever it is, it can't be that bad. Verity can help."

"No! We can't tell Verity, she might kick me off the team."

Severina explained how she couldn't resist taking a peek in a shiny box that was tucked right up in the corner of the storage cupboard.

"I didn't realise what I'd done at first. I looked inside and heard a little voice shouting, 'I'm free!' and thanking me, as a whoosh of cold air blew past."

"What was in the box?" Autumn asked, wondering if there really was a gym ghost after all.

"I don't know – it was invisible!" Severina cried. "It wasn't until strange things started happening in the gym that I realised it must be whatever was in that box. I was too scared to say anything in case I got into trouble or was kicked off the team."

"It's OK," Autumn said. "At least you've told me now, and there's no real harm done."

"Except for our water bottles – yuk!" said Leif, scrunching his nose up.

Autumn and Severina jumped as they realised the rest of Black Cats had been listening by the door.

"Yeah, don't worry, we can sort this," said Batty, and the team murmured in agreement.

"I've been thinking about this, and I think I know what to do to reveal who or what is making all these strange things happen." Autumn told everyone her plan. "We need to be absolutely focused on dance and move in harmony as a team and I think it might just work."

The Black Cats team members arranged themselves ready to dance.

"Music will really help us focus," Autumn said.

"Leave it to me." Leif swished his wand and music blasted out from unseen speakers.

The Black cats danced, cartwheeled and flipped across the mats in perfect harmony until silver glitter and snowflakes fluttered above them. The pictures on the wall spun in circles and loud raspberry blowing noises could just be heard over the music, but this time the team kept on dancing.

As the dance continued, the smell of cinnamon wafted through the air and the gym filled with a layer of snow. Soon a figure emerged as the settled snowflakes revealed an invisible outline

The dance came to an end and Autumn gasped when she spotted the snow-covered figure twinkling with magic.

We did it, Autumn thought. *We've found the culprit.*

Verity clapped and whooped from by the door, while mugs, filled with a delicious-smelling green and brown drink with star sprinkles twinkling on top, floated in the air behind her. The mugs slowly landed on a table in the corner of the gym. "Well, that was just extraordinary! And I see we have discovered an extra guest for our sleepover."

All eyes were on the not-so-invisible figure; it wasn't a gym ghost after all. It was a pixie!

Autumn and Severina explained to Verity what had happened and how the pixie had ended up at the gym.

"Some of those boxes have been in the storage cupboard since we moved in here,"

Verity said. "The poor pixie could have been trapped for years."

"Can you speak?" Autumn asked the pixie.

"I can, but my voice is only little, so nobody ever notices me," squeaked the pixie. "That's how I got trapped in the first place; nobody could hear me shouting that I'd got stuck in there."

"That's the voice I heard when I looked in the box," Severina said.

"And I can't thank you enough for letting me out," the snow-covered pixie said, smiling.

"Let me try a spell." Verity took her wand out and formed a figure of eight and chanted, "*Little and tiny, let your voice become mighty!*"

When the pixie spoke again, everyone could hear her clearly. "Thank you so much!"

"Why did you keep messing with things in the gym and playing tricks on us when we were dancing?" Autumn asked.

"I was just trying to get everyone's attention, but also I was a bit jealous because I've always wanted to dance. I got a bit carried away." The pixie looked at the floor and avoided everyone's eyes.

"That's OK," Autumn said.

"It was so lonely being stuck in a box. I'm just so happy to see people again and wanted to be friends."

The pixie looked at Severina. "Thank you for freeing me. If you hadn't peeked inside the box, I could have been trapped for ever!"

Severina's cheeks turned pink.

"It's been so nice to see you all dance, I really love dancing." The pixie twirled and the magical snowflakes and silver sparkles that were still on her shimmered. She stopped and looked around at everyone. "I'm sorry I caused so much trouble."

"It was fun, really," Skye said, grinning, and the other teammates agreed.

"It's made this the best magical mystery spooky sleepover ever!" said Leif.

"Well, you're more than welcome to stay here as long as you want," said Verity. "You can come and dance with us whenever you like."

"That would be wonderful, thank you so much!" the pixie said.

"Now that's all settled, you'd better have your

snot chocolates before they go cold." Verity pointed
to the steaming mugs on the table.

The teammates all grabbed a mug and Autumn gulped down her drink, thirsty after all the dancing. The delicious warmth of the snot chocolate spread through her body, giving her a happy glow.

"You look like you've got a silver moustache," Batty laughed.

"You do too!" said Autumn.

Autumn wiped star sprinkles from her mouth and smiled as she looked round at her friends. *I'm so glad to be part of Black Cats,* she thought.

"I guess it's like Rainbow always says, I'm putting the sparkle in Sparkledale!"

 **THE END**

LEARN TO DANCE LIKE AUTUMN!

Follow the steps below to dance like Autumn.

Dance warning – magic may happen!

Make sure you practice somewhere with
plenty of space around you and where
noone will bump into you.

5

6

7

8

HAVE YOU READ AUTUMN'S FIRST ADVENTURE?

AUTUMN
MOONBEAM

DANCE MAGIC!

EMMA FINLAYSON-PALMER & HEIDI CANNON

ACKNOWLEDGEMENTS

There are so many people that help along the way in making a book, there's a whole community of Team Autumn Moonbeam out there, I'm so sorry if I've missed anyone, but know I value and love you all!

Thank you so much to Hazel Holmes for believing in Autumn and me enough to bring her back for another adventure. Thanks also to Charlotte and the whole UCLan team and students, Becky Chilcott's amazing designs, Kathy Webb's fabulous edits, Graeme Williams, and everyone else who has played a part in making my dreams come true.

Huge thanks to Heidi Cannon, whose beautiful illustrations brought Autumn's world to life and never cease to amaze me in how stunning they are!

Special thanks to Veronique Baxter, my lovely agent and the amazing team at the David Higham agency for all you do. And to Laura West for starting Autumn's journey with me.

To Carolyn Ward, Tizzie Frankish, and Amy Feest, a HUGE thank you for all your hand holding and generally being fabulous friends and excellent editors.

Ashley Haffie-Hobday, Susan Mann, Melissa Welliver, Emily Randall, Emma Bradley, Eiman Munro, Anne Boyere, Tamsyn Murray, Tash Holmes, Jeanna Skinner, Lorna Riley and Anna Orridge for always cheering me on and being lovely, supportive friends.

Elizabeth Hardie and Jen Rigby for your endless support and friendship over the years.

Thank you to my lovely writing friends, Tamsin Rosewell and Kennilworth Books, the #ukteenchat gang, online writing groups, especially The Nearlies, my Debut 22 group, the SCBWI Central West crit group, Write MAGIC, Amie and Charlie at Urban Writers' Retreat, Castlecroft Writers, and Wombourne Writers, staff and friends at Castlecroft Primary School, NAWG, Stuart White and everyone involved in the fabulous #WriteMentor community, Northern Gravy, PaperBound Magazine, Book Jive Live, and so many lovely people that have been part of this journey!

Massive thanks to all the indie bookshops, bloggers, reviewers, teachers, podcasters, and everyone who has championed my stories, you are all stars! And a special shout out to my local bookshops Wolverhampton Waterstones, and Blue Sheep Books in Wednesbury.

Thank you to the Sharon Ann Academy of Cheer and Dance; for being the source of inspiration that sparked Autumn's creation.

Thank you to my Mom and Dad, sister, Hazel, and brother-in-law, Liam, for all your support and help.

A HUGE thank you to my husband, Alex, my biggest supporter, and best friend, and to my amazing children, who are always my inspiration.